The Big Stone

"Who cares about apathy?"
— My father, Thomas Charles Garland, circa 1968

"What's for dinner?"
— My son, Kevin Michael Garland, circa lunchtime

Published by The Millbrook Press, Inc.
2 Old New Milford Road
Brookfield, Connecticut 06804

Library of Congress Cataloging-in-Publication Data
Garland, Michael, 1952-
The big stone / Michael Garland.
p. cm.
Summary: After having watched his father live a life of regrets while
saddled with a huge stone he feels he must carry around with him, a
son finds happiness by choosing to follow his own path rather than that
of his father's.
ISBN 0-7613-1261-7 (lib. bdg.)
[1. Fathers and sons—Fiction. 2. Individuality—Fiction.]
I. Title.
PZ7.G18413Bi 1999
[Fic]—dc21   98-46386   CIP   AC

The Big Stone

Michael Garland

THE MILLBROOK PRESS
Brookfield, Connecticut

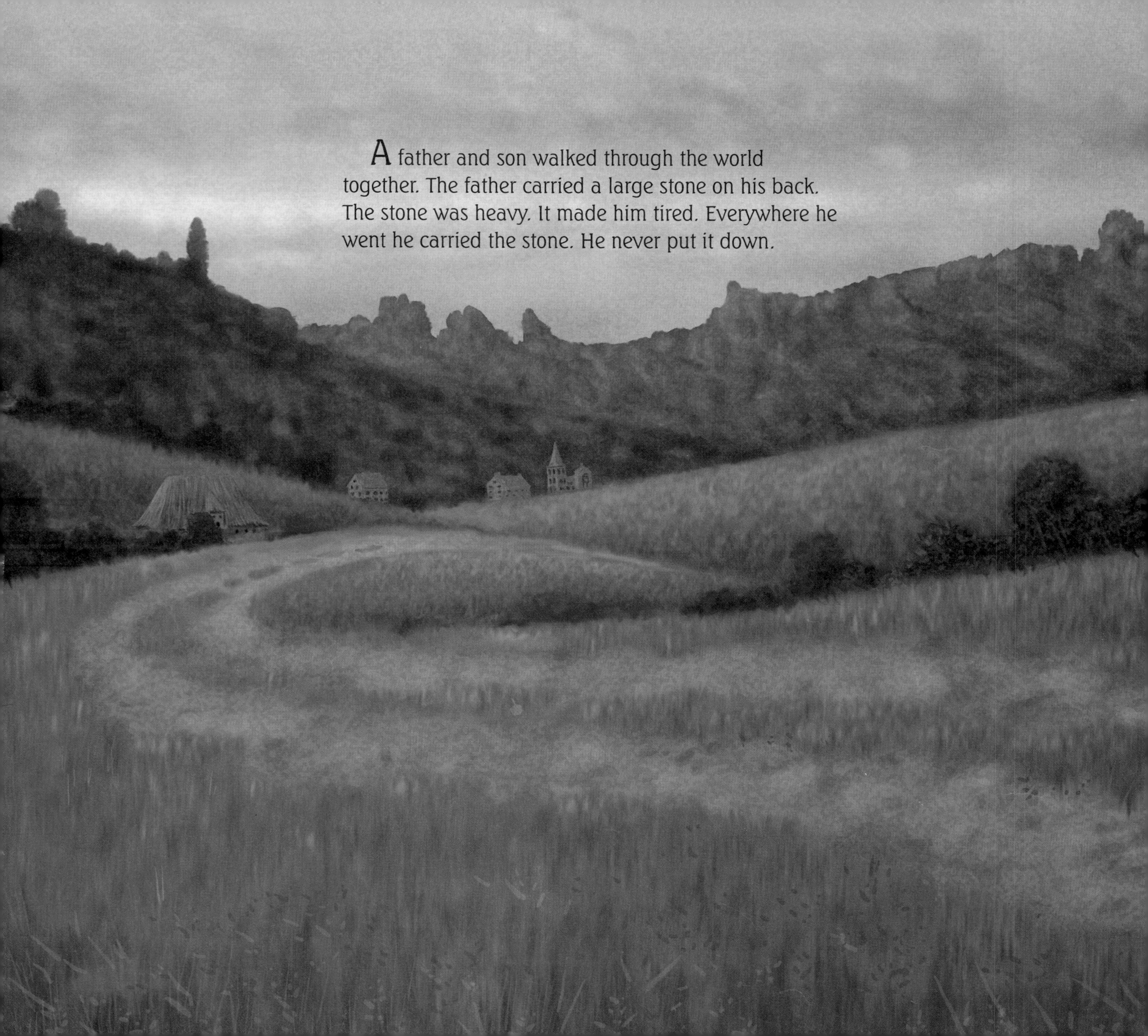

A father and son walked through the world together. The father carried a large stone on his back. The stone was heavy. It made him tired. Everywhere he went he carried the stone. He never put it down.

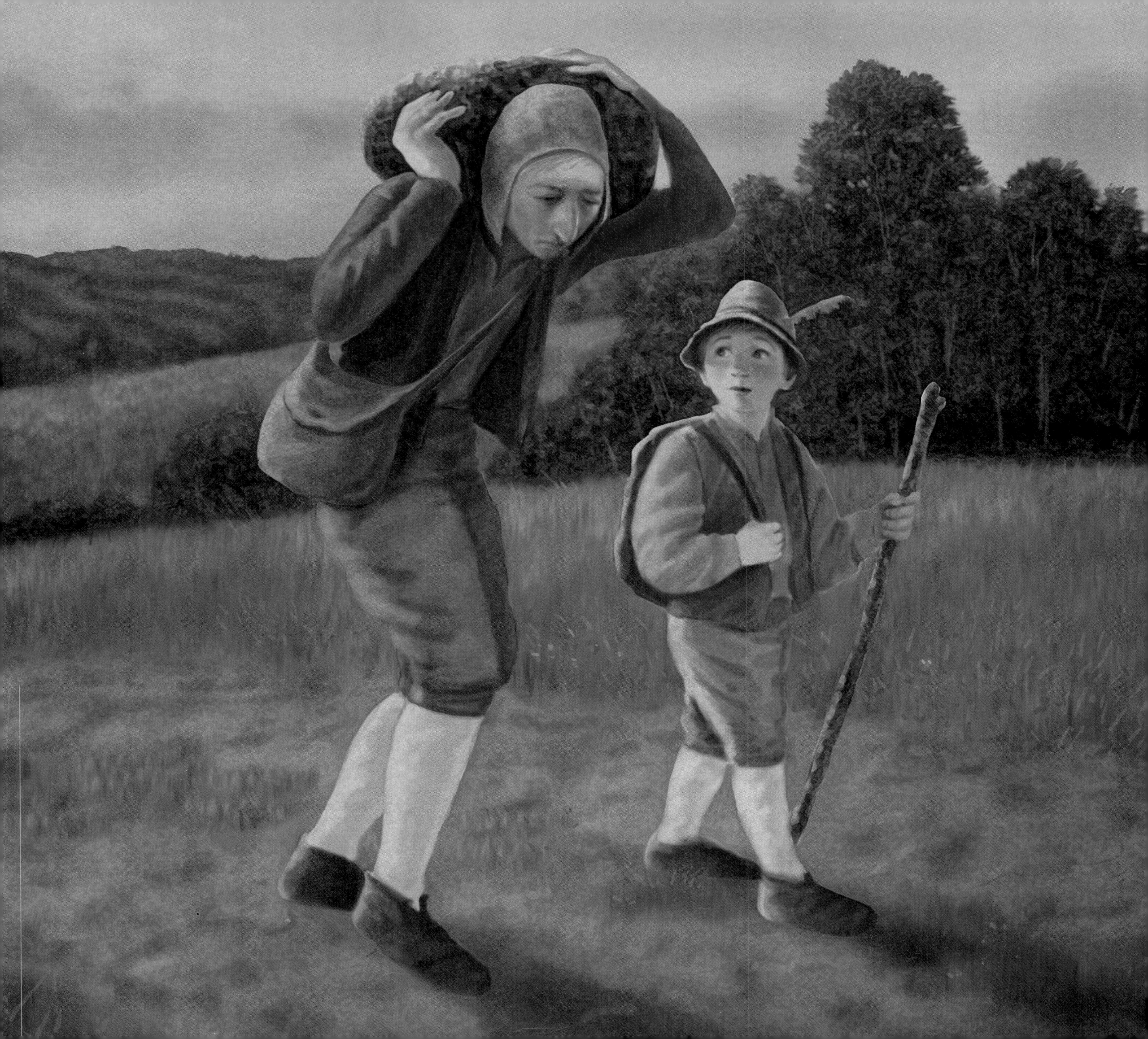

The father and son had almost nothing but the clothes they wore. The father would do odd jobs, here and there, or beg. They lived from hand to mouth.

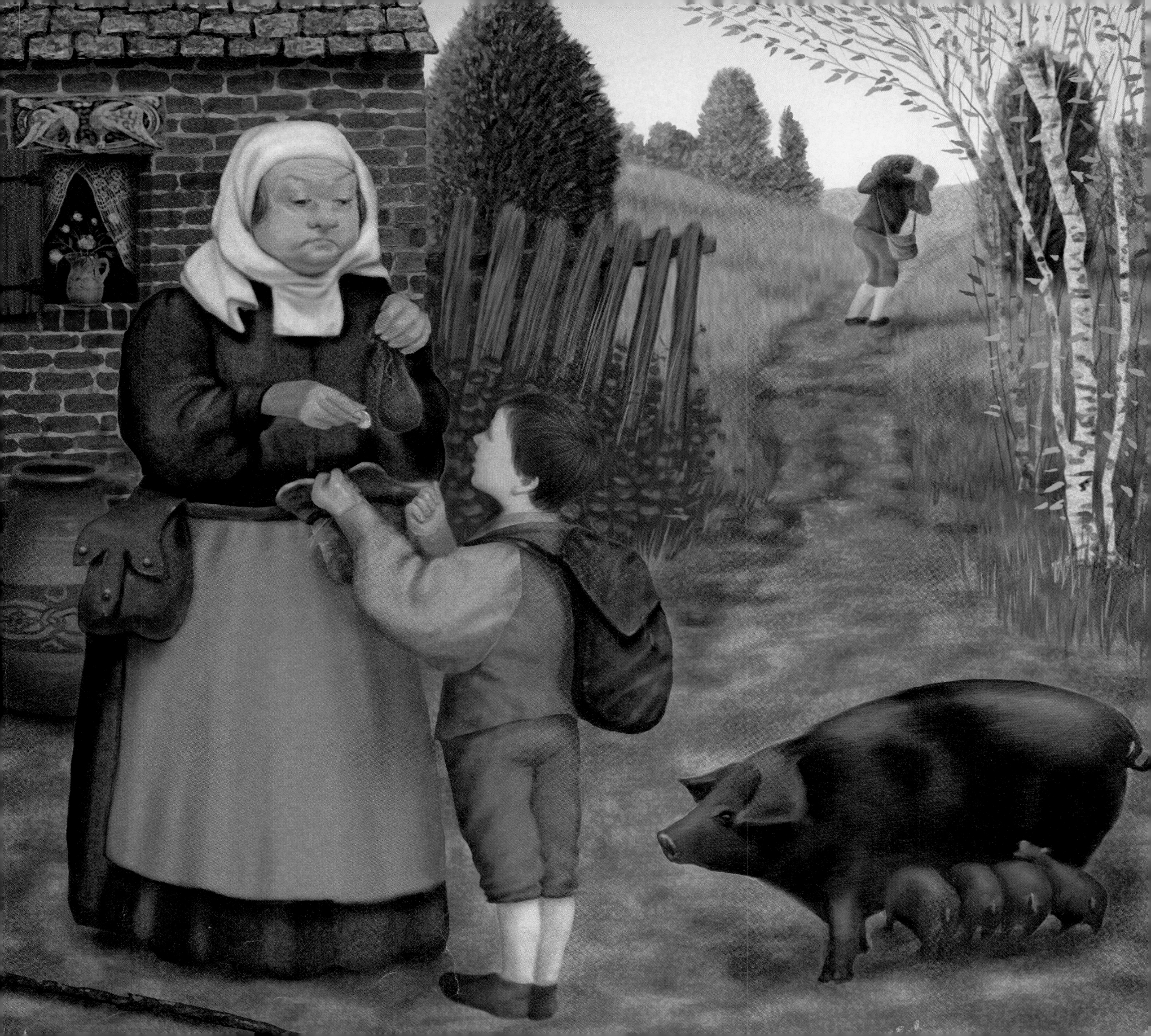

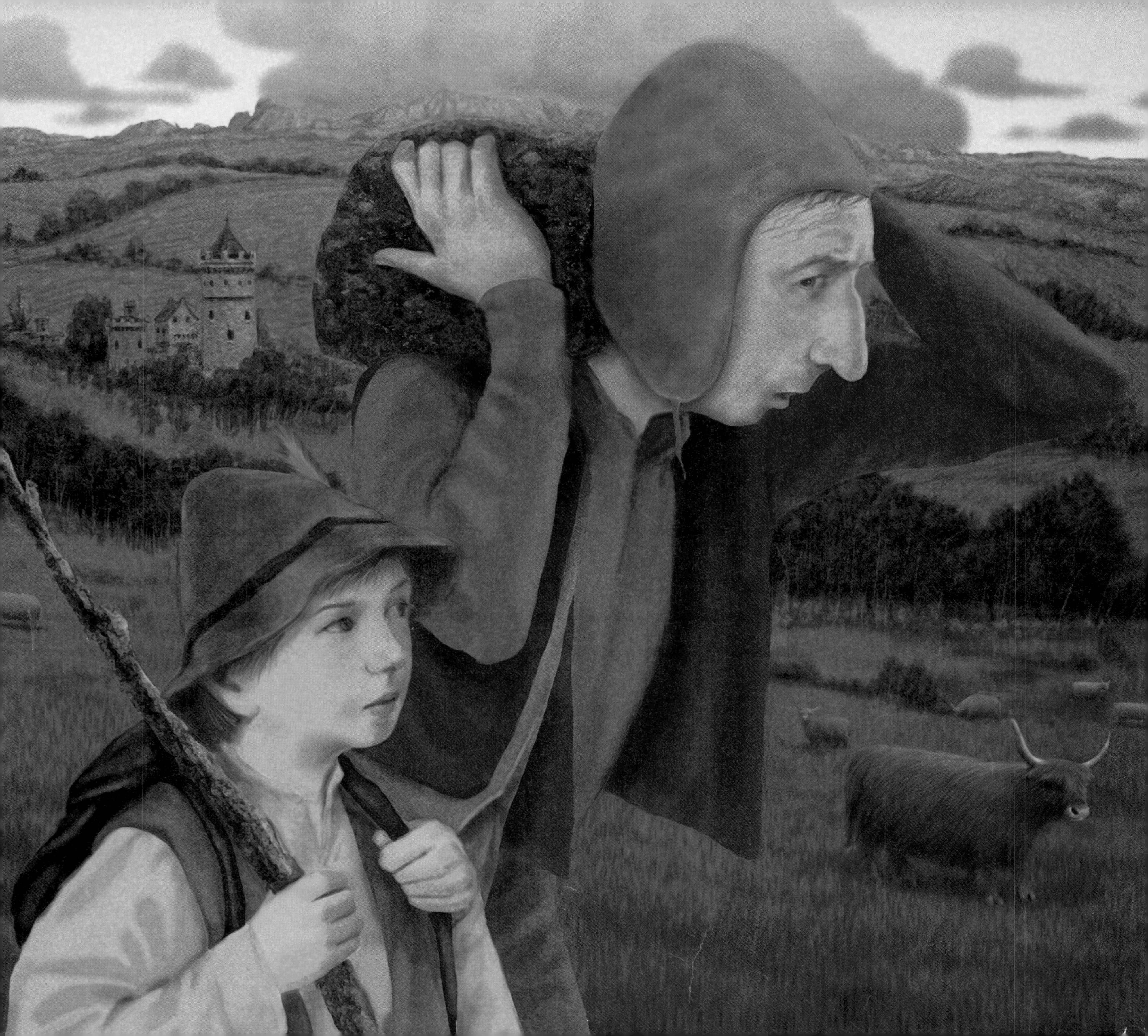

The son could not remember a time when his father did not carry the stone. One day while walking up a steep hill, the son thought to ask. "Father, why do you carry the stone?"

"Because I have to," wheezed the father. "My father gave it to me."

"Where did he get it?" was the son's next question.

"His father gave it to him."

"Have you asked anyone to help you?" the boy inquired.

"Again and again, but no one had the time to help, so I stopped asking," replied the father.

"When I am bigger I will help!" the son promised, as they trudged up the hill together.

Sometimes the son walked ahead of his father and asked people to help. He saw a shepherd and asked, "Will you help my father carry his heavy stone?"

"No, I can't. I have my flock to tend," the shepherd said.

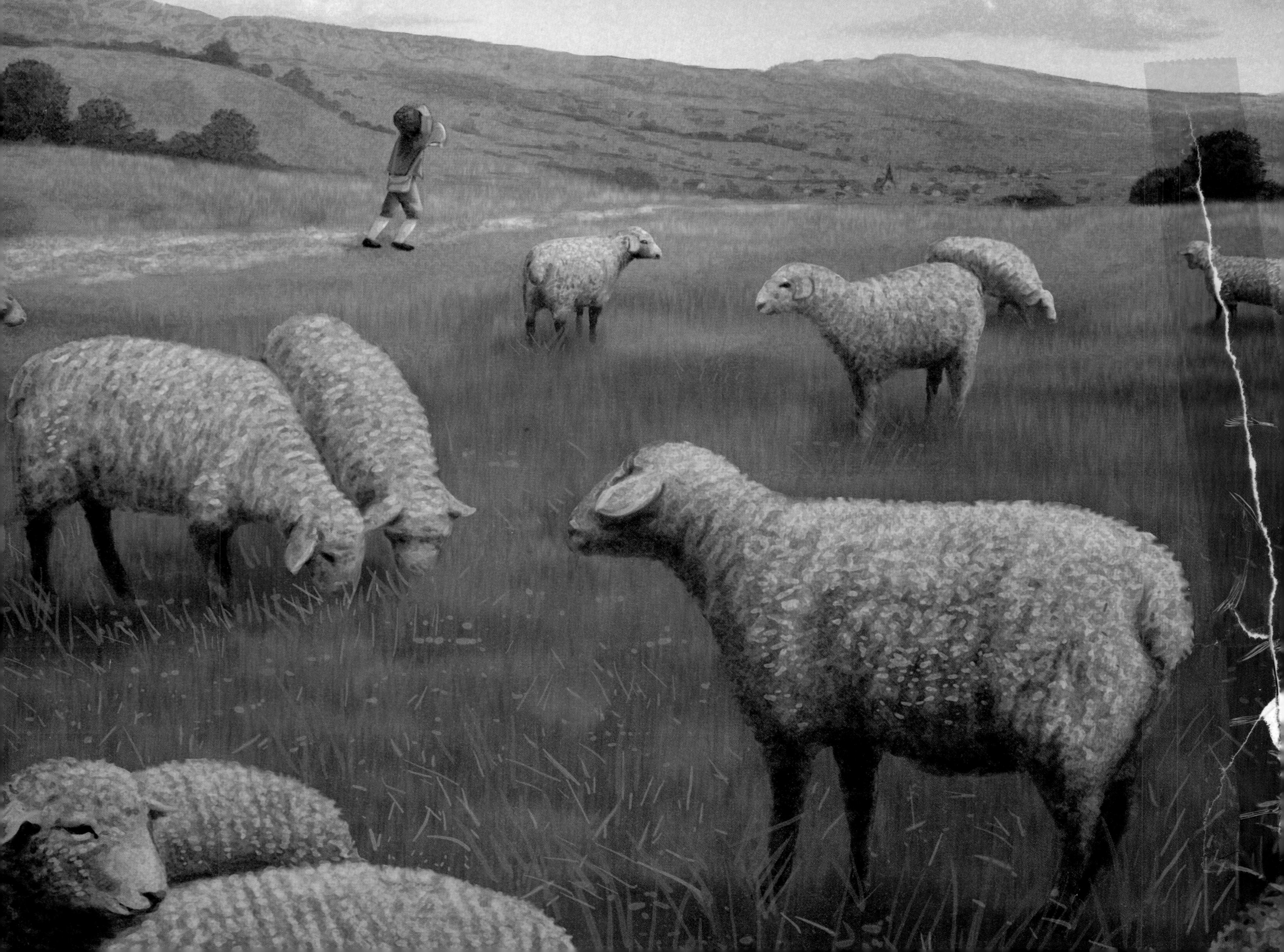

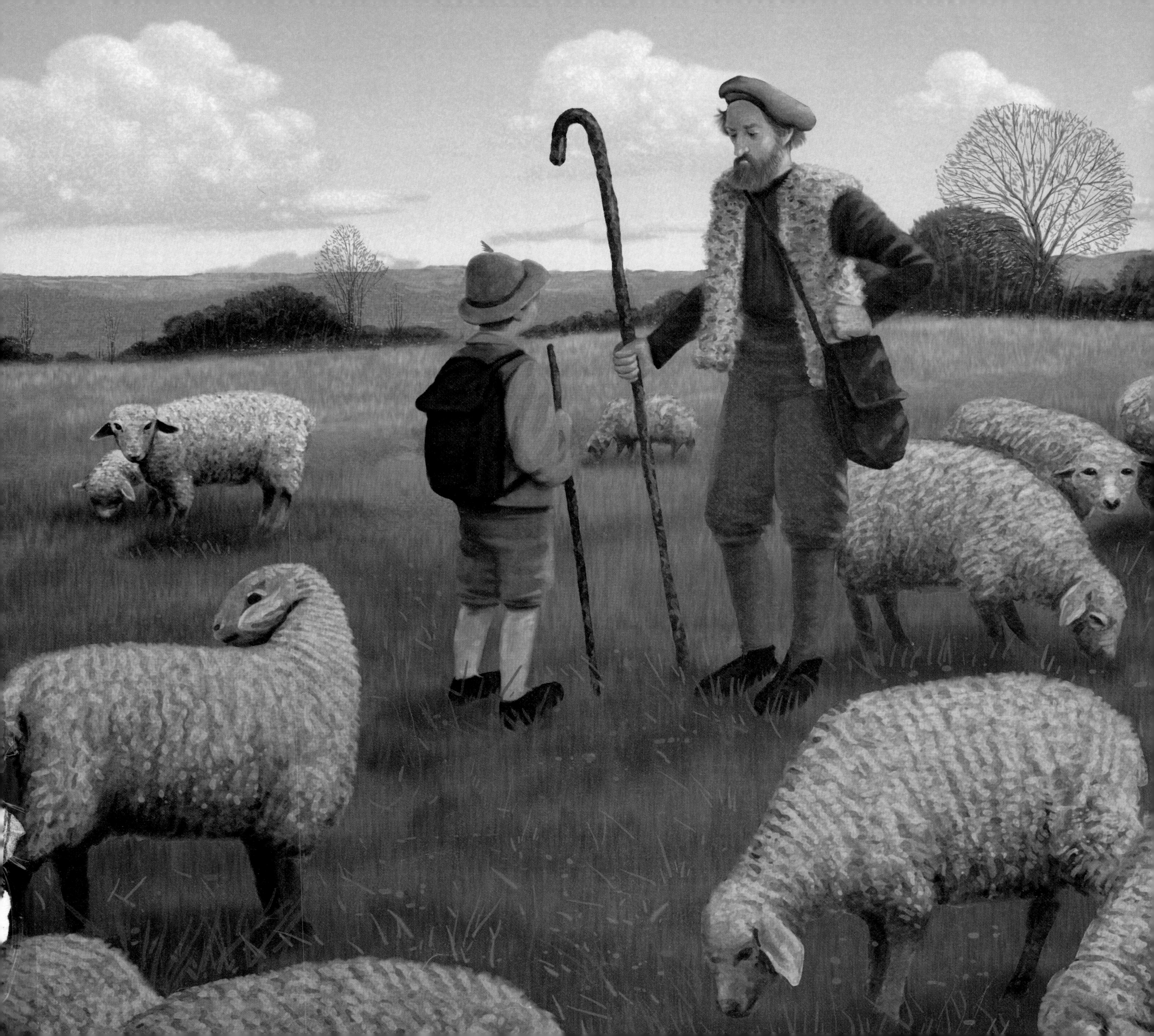

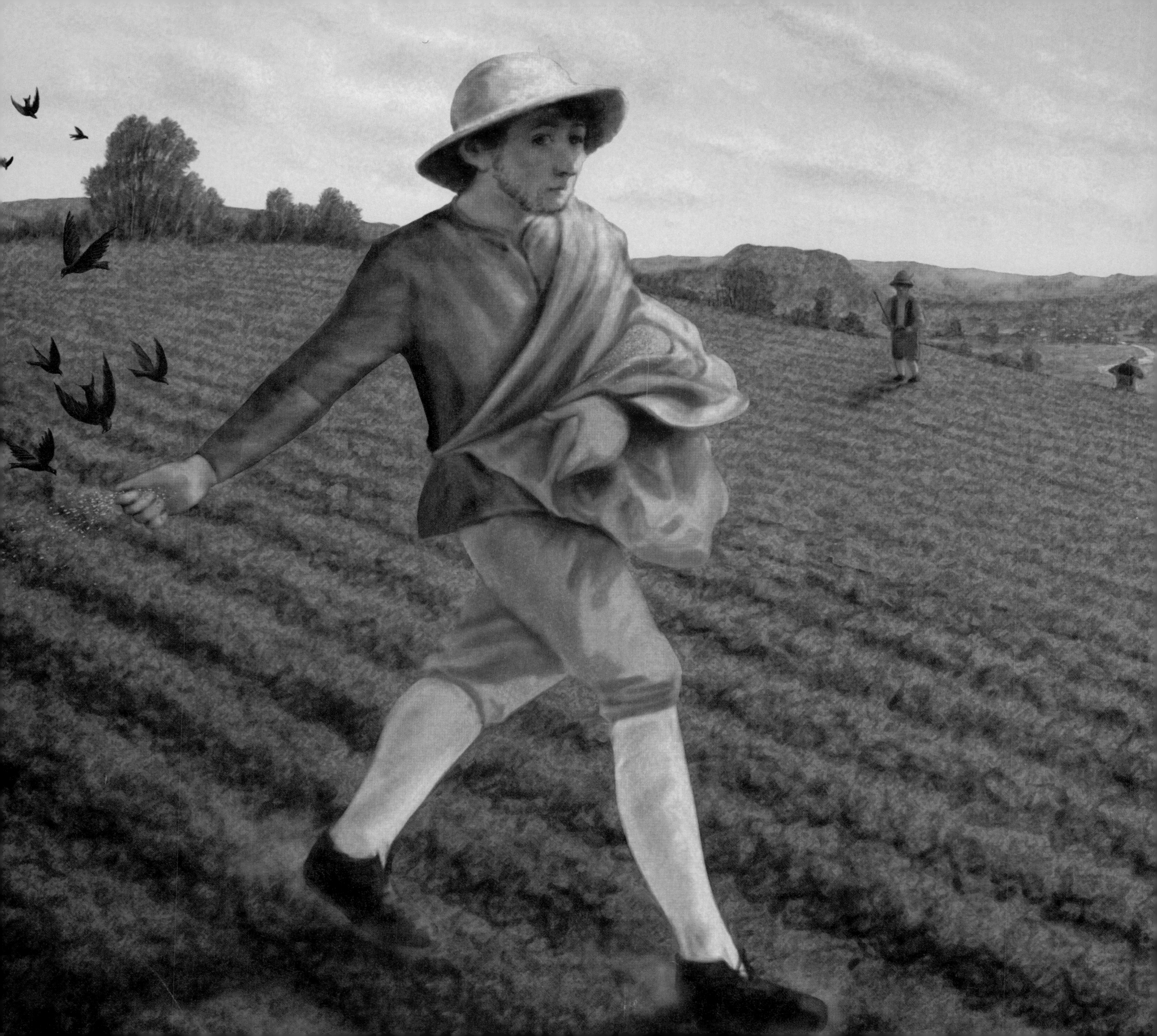

The boy came upon a farmer, and asked,
"Can you help my father with his heavy load?"
"I am too busy sowing my fields with seed,"
the farmer said.

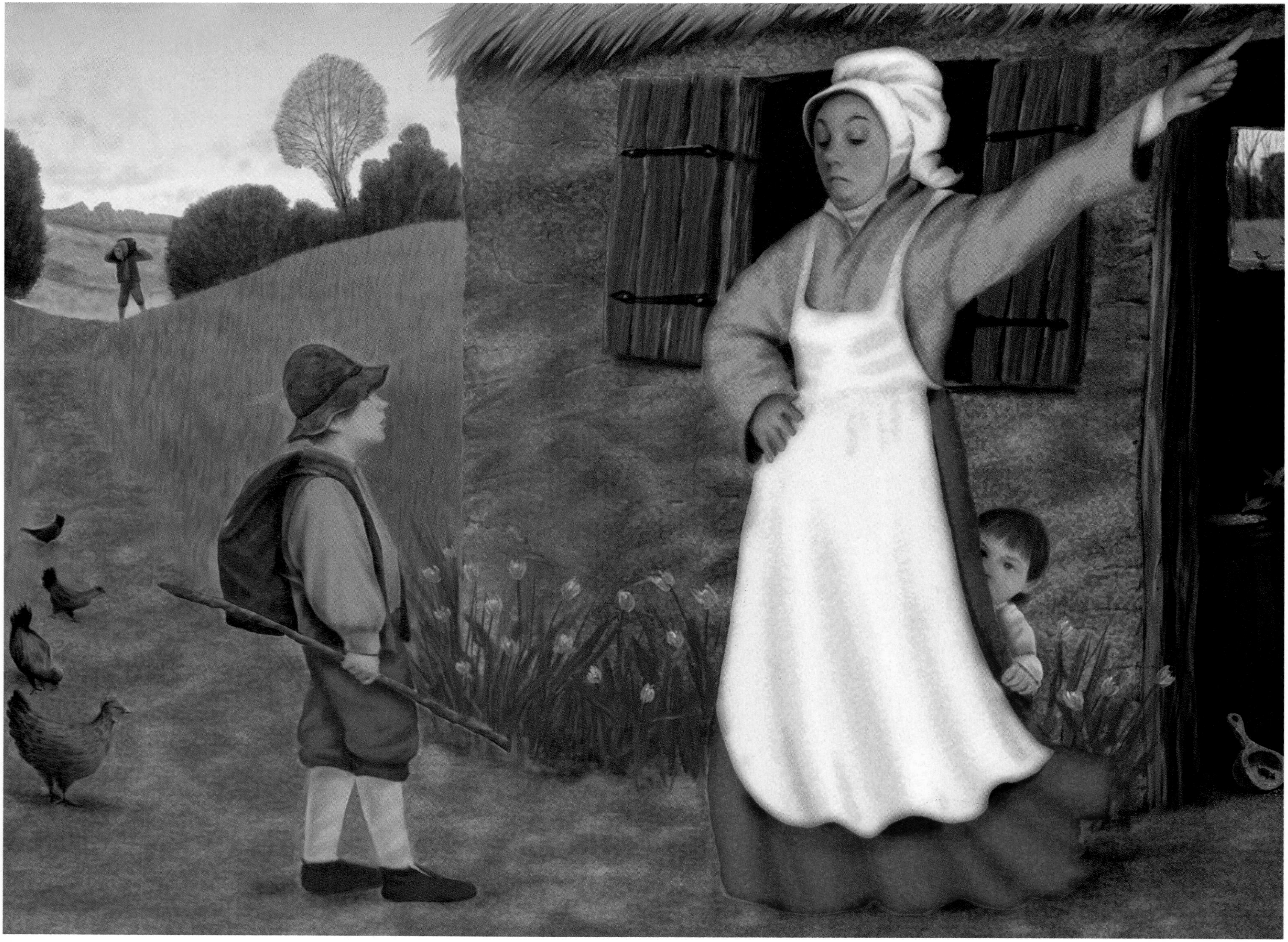

Next the boy asked the farmer's wife. She shook her head. "If I help you, who will clean my house and take care of my children?"

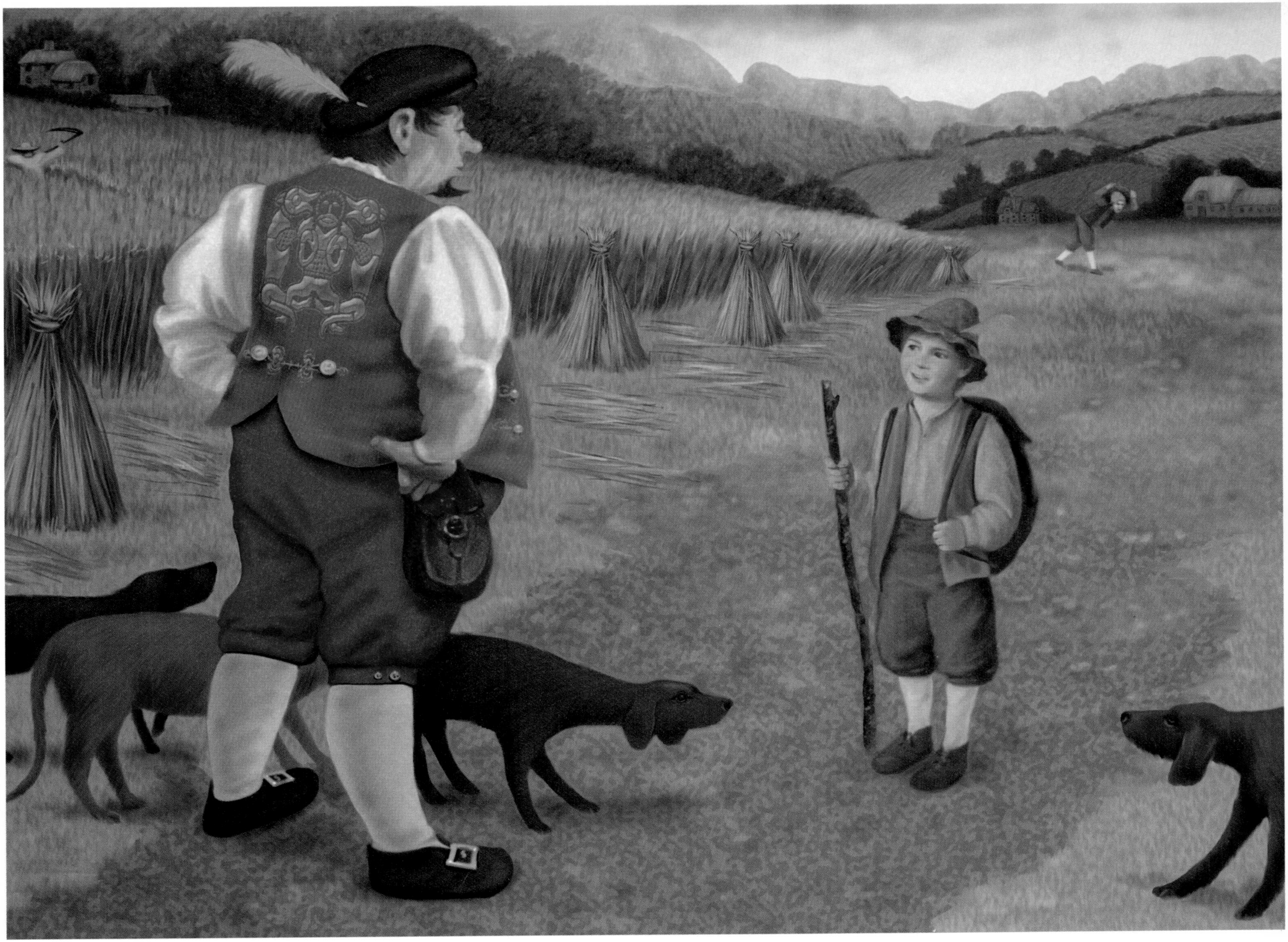

Then the boy met a rich merchant who said, "Time is money, and I have precious little to spend on you!"

Soon the boy realized that his father had been right. And he, too, gave up asking people for help.

Sometimes, while they were resting from their journey or hiding from bad weather, the father would tell his son about all the things he could have done, if he did not have to carry his stone around.

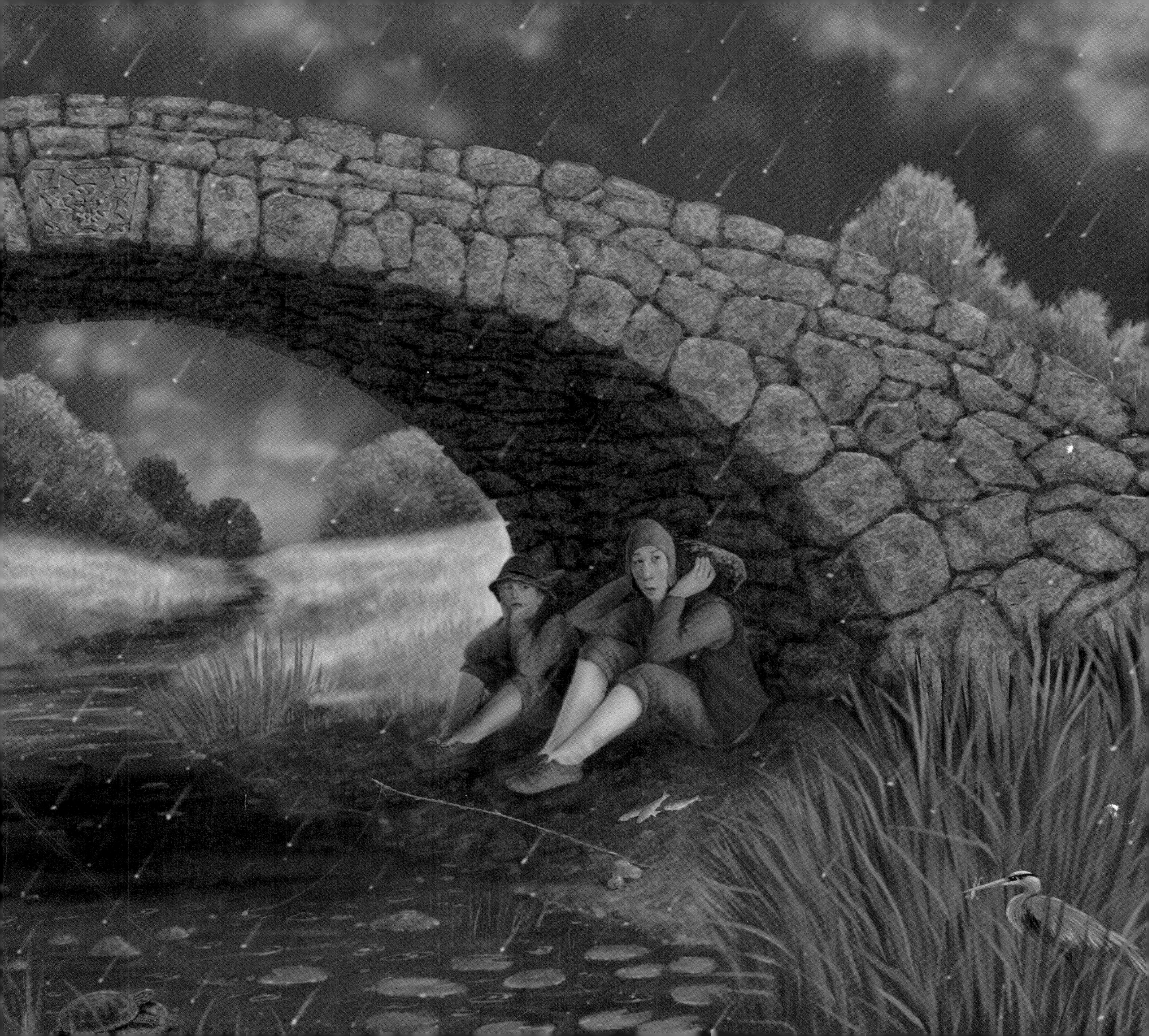

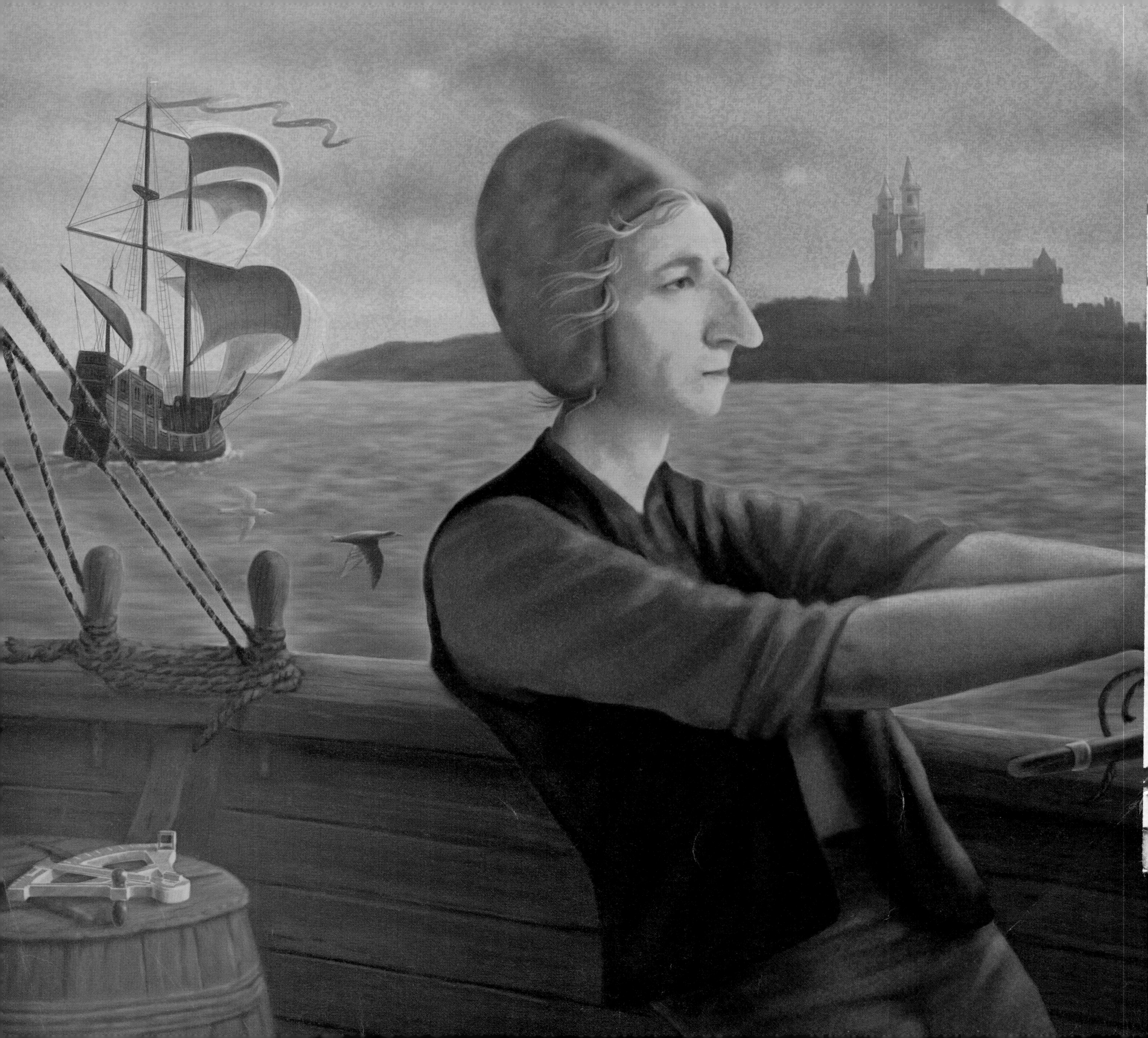

The father said, "I could have been a sailor and sailed to far-off lands, and seen many beautiful things."

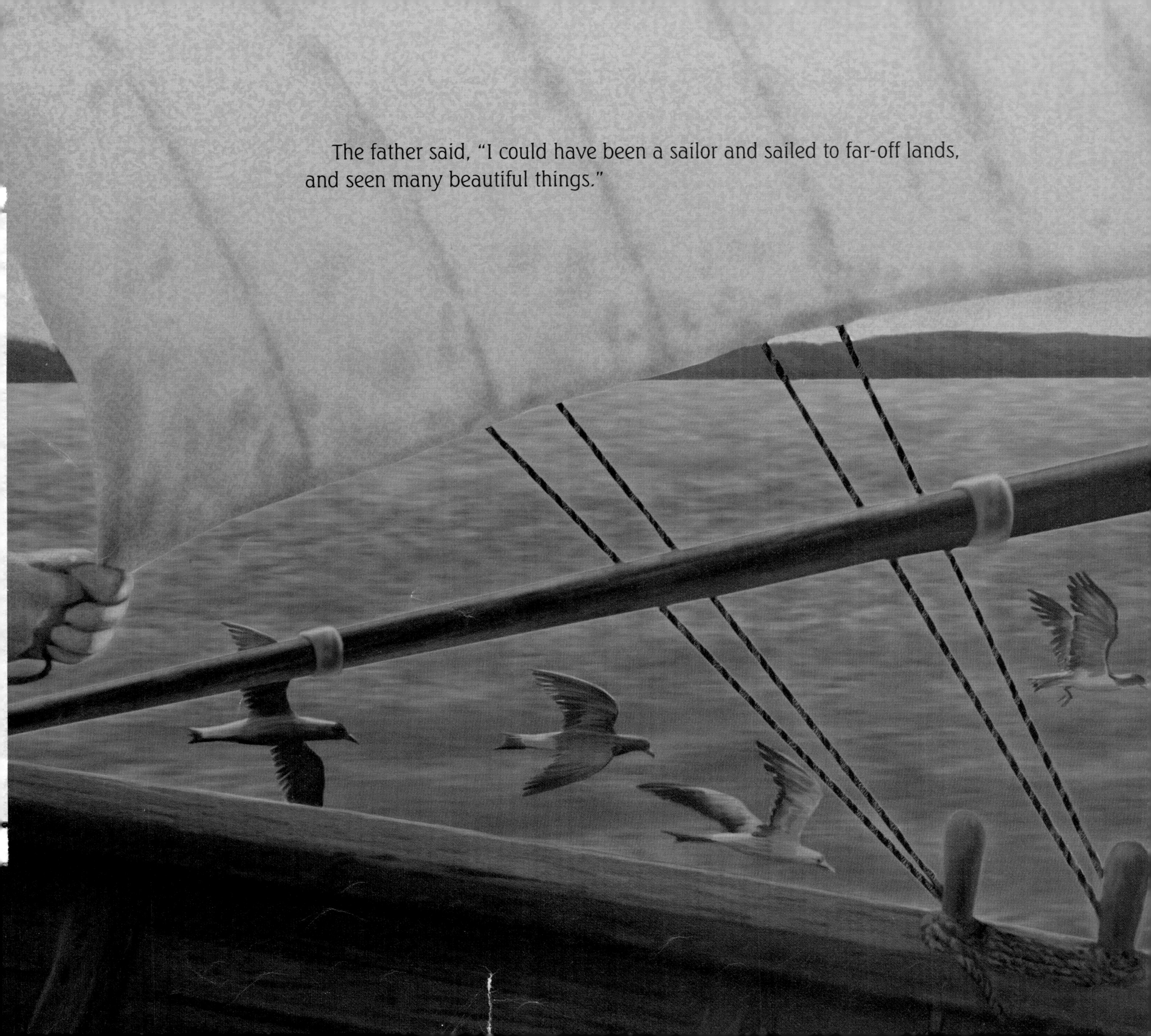

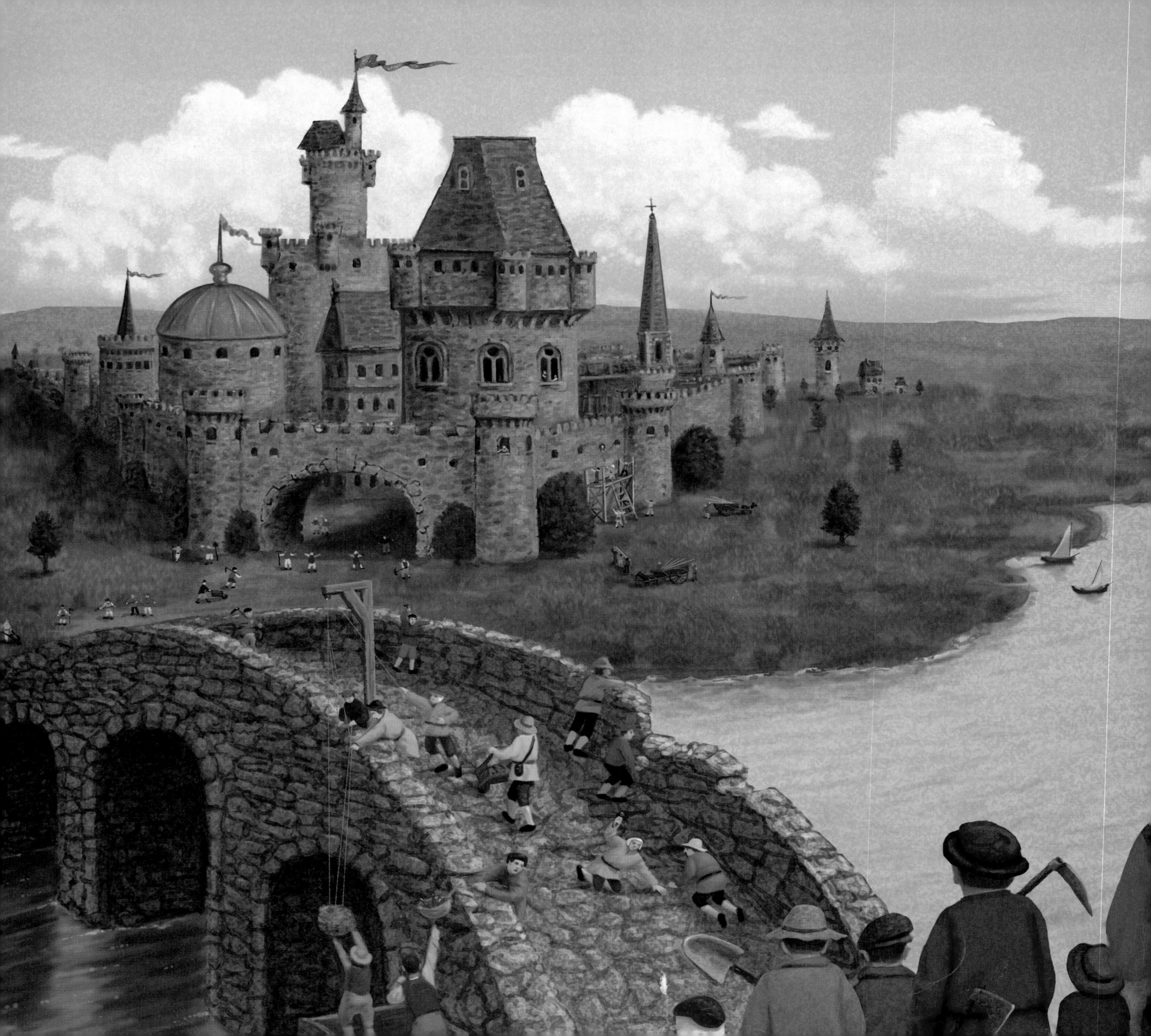

"I could have been a builder. I could have made bridges and castles and great churches."

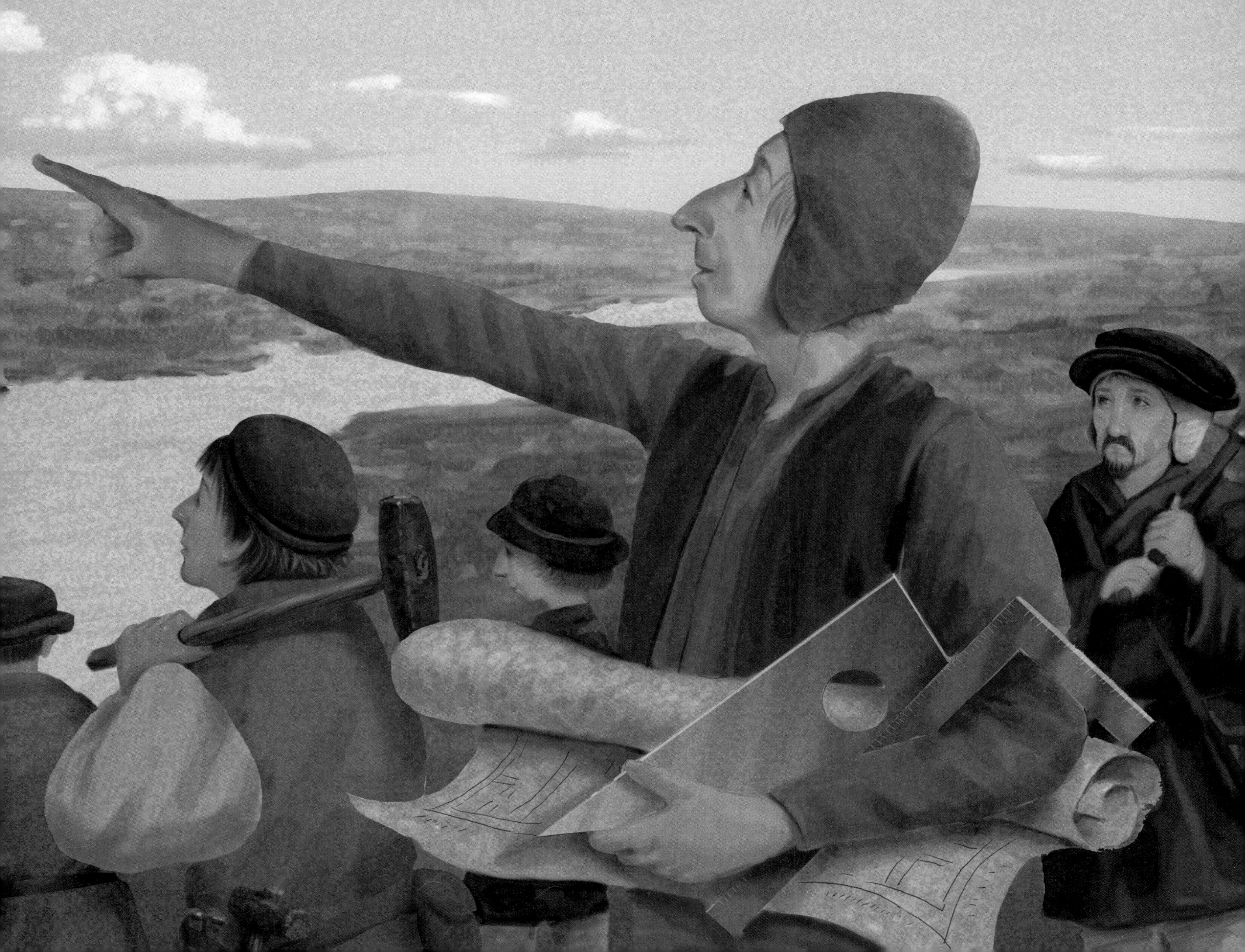

The father would go on and on like that for hours, but he always ended with the same thing.

"If it wasn't for this stone," he said, with tears forming in his eyes, "I could have loved your mother more. And she would not have died of a broken heart."

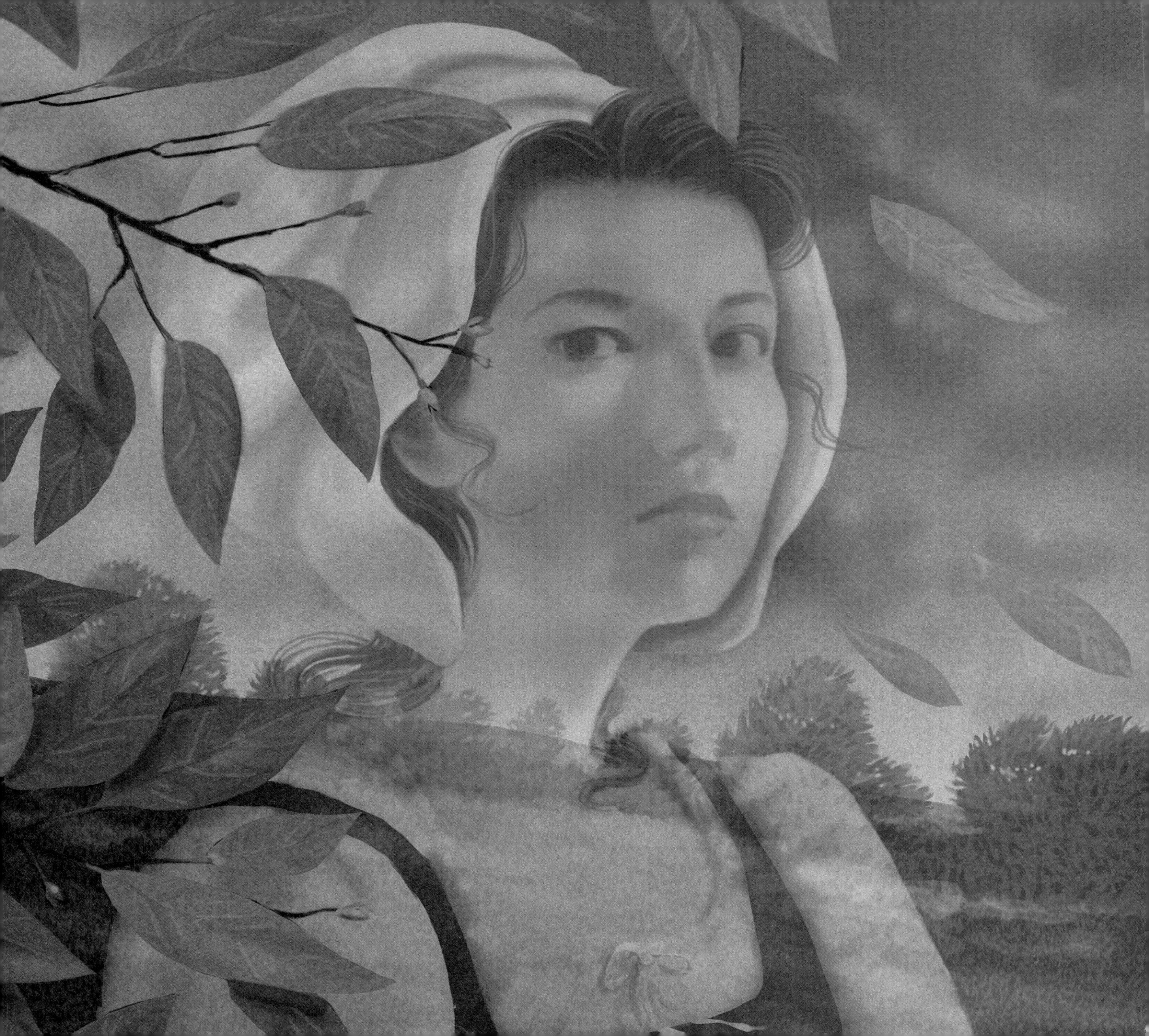

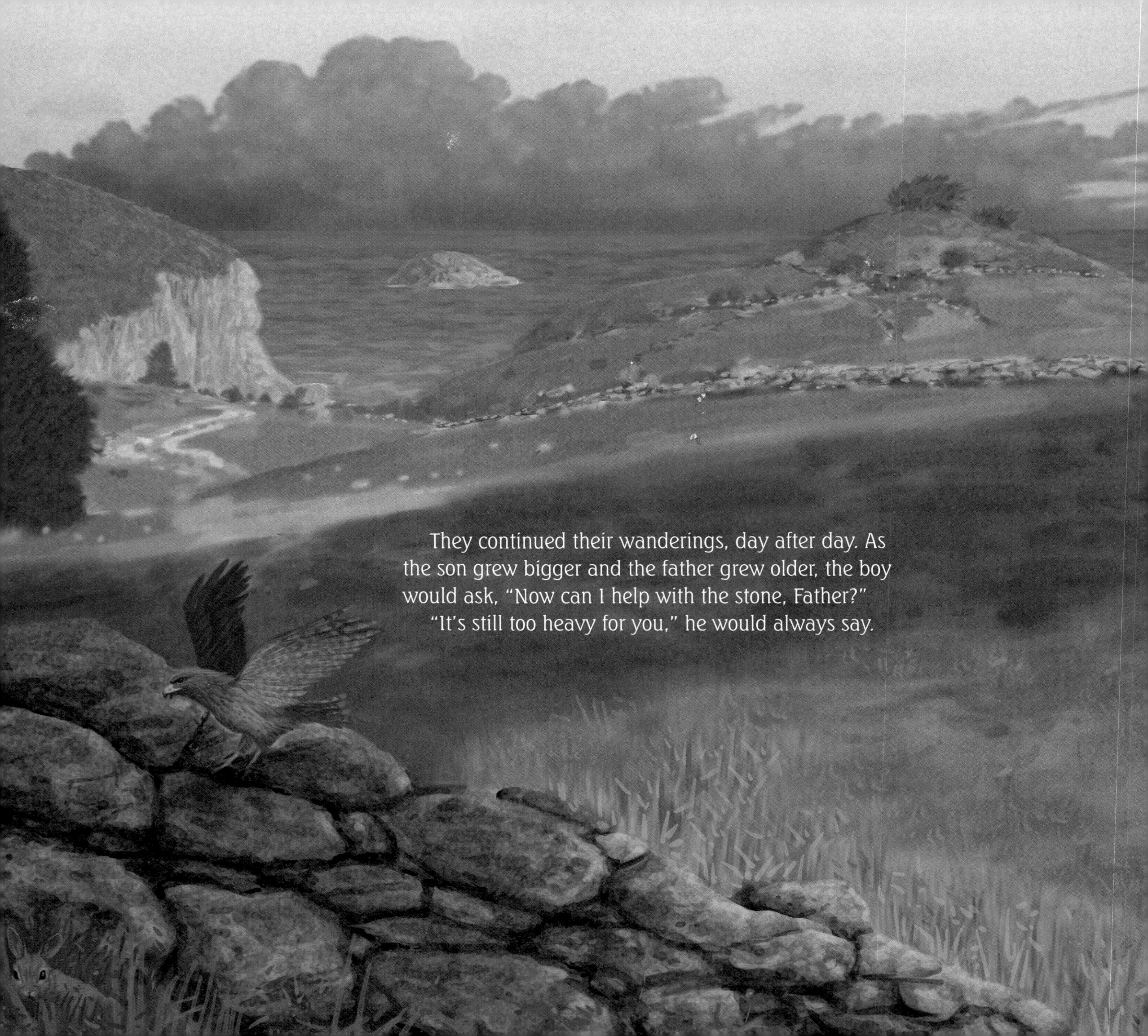

They continued their wanderings, day after day. As the son grew bigger and the father grew older, the boy would ask, "Now can I help with the stone, Father?"

"It's still too heavy for you," he would always say.

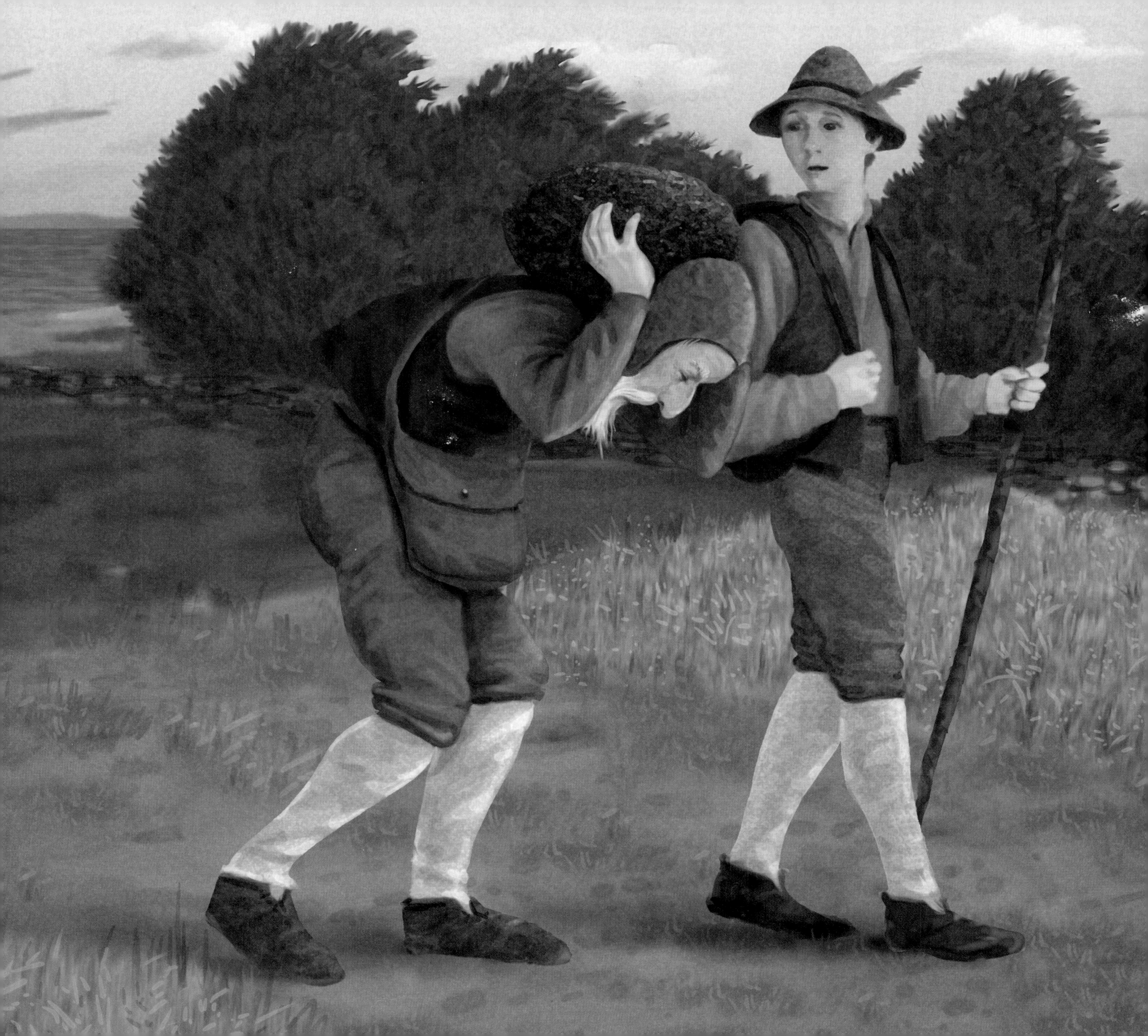

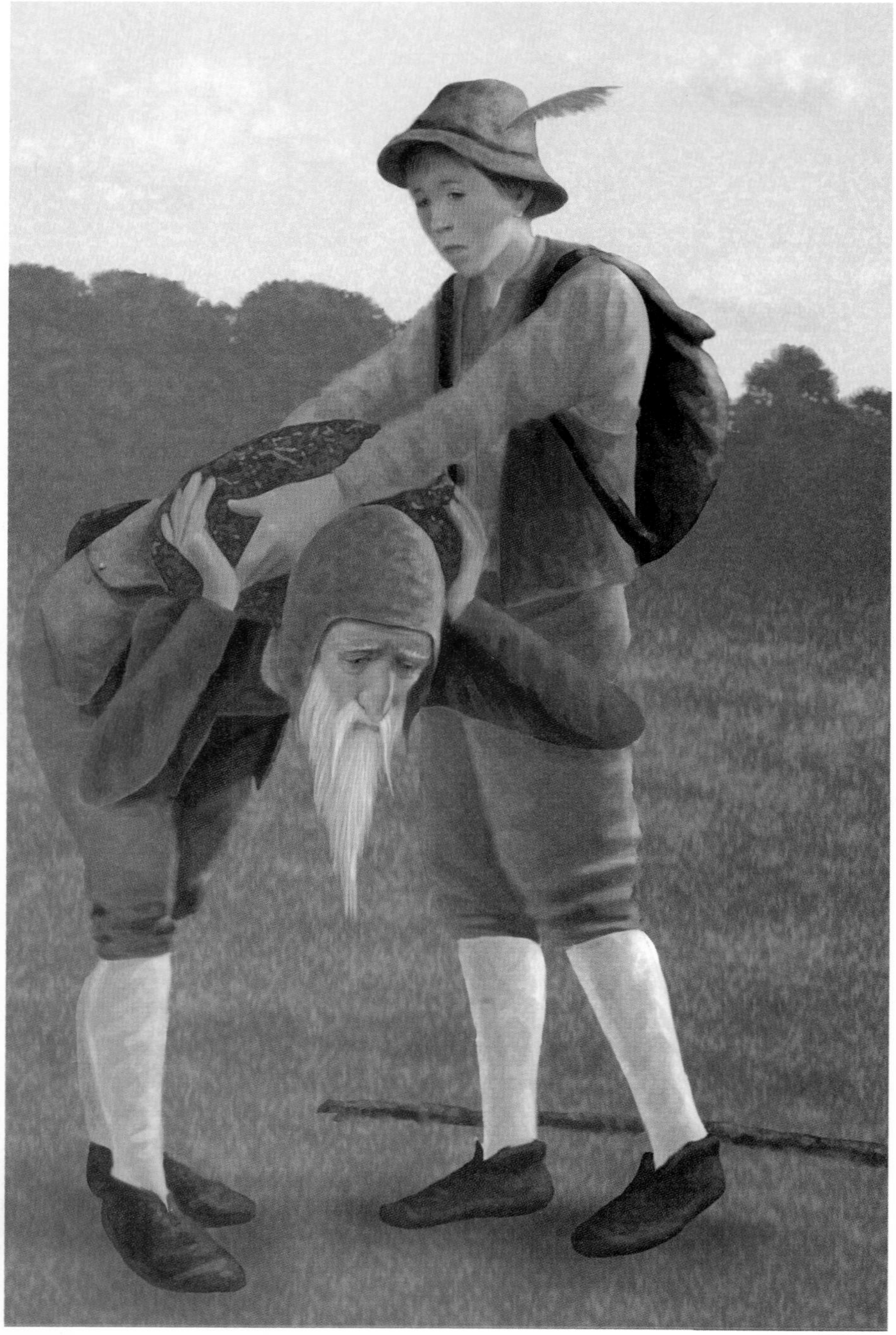

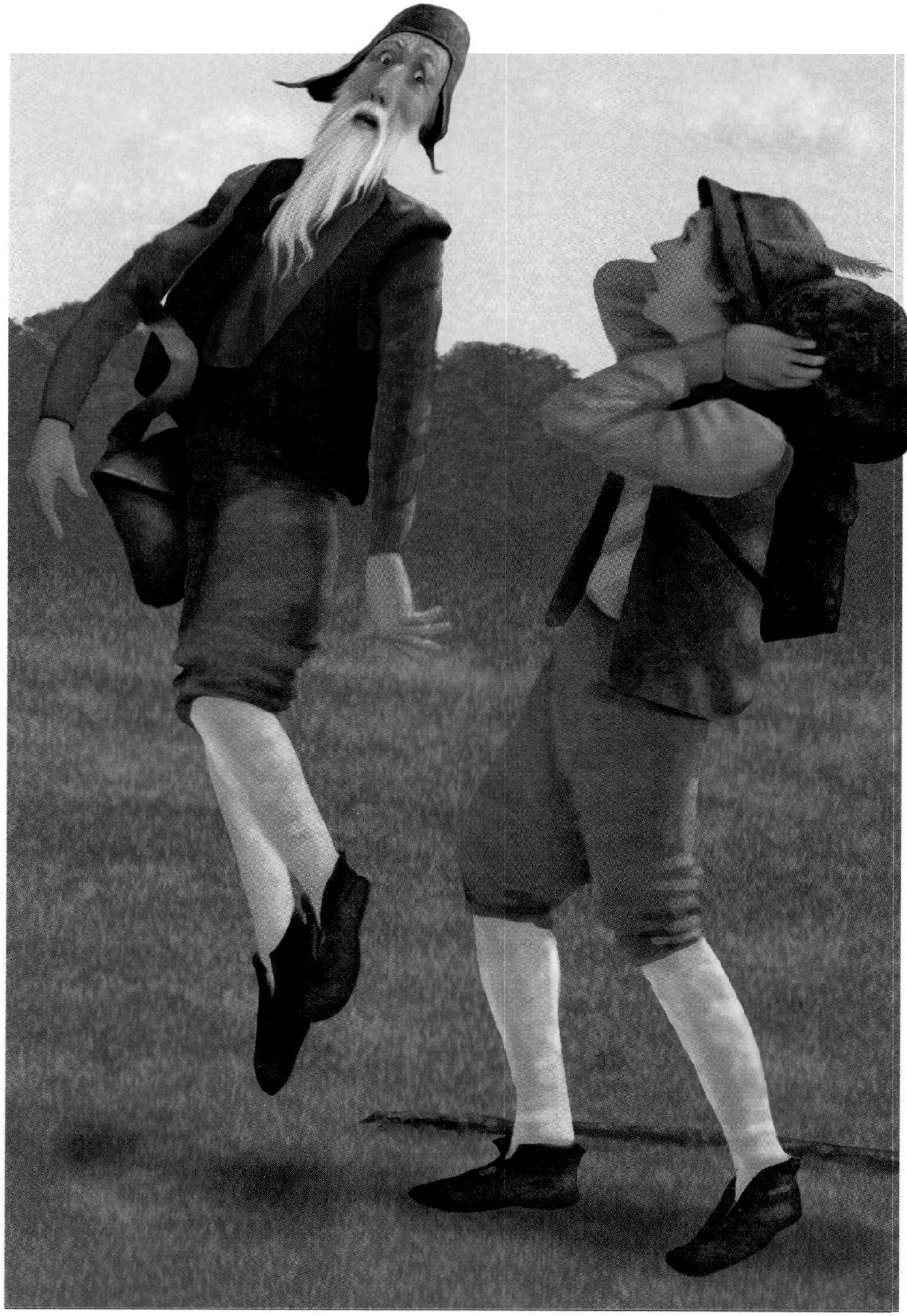

The day came when the father could not take another step. Without saying anything, the son gently lifted the heavy stone from his father's back and put it on his own. With no weight on his back the father could straighten up for the first time. He had a look of great wonderment to feel the lightness on his feet. He was so light, in fact, that he started to float in the air.

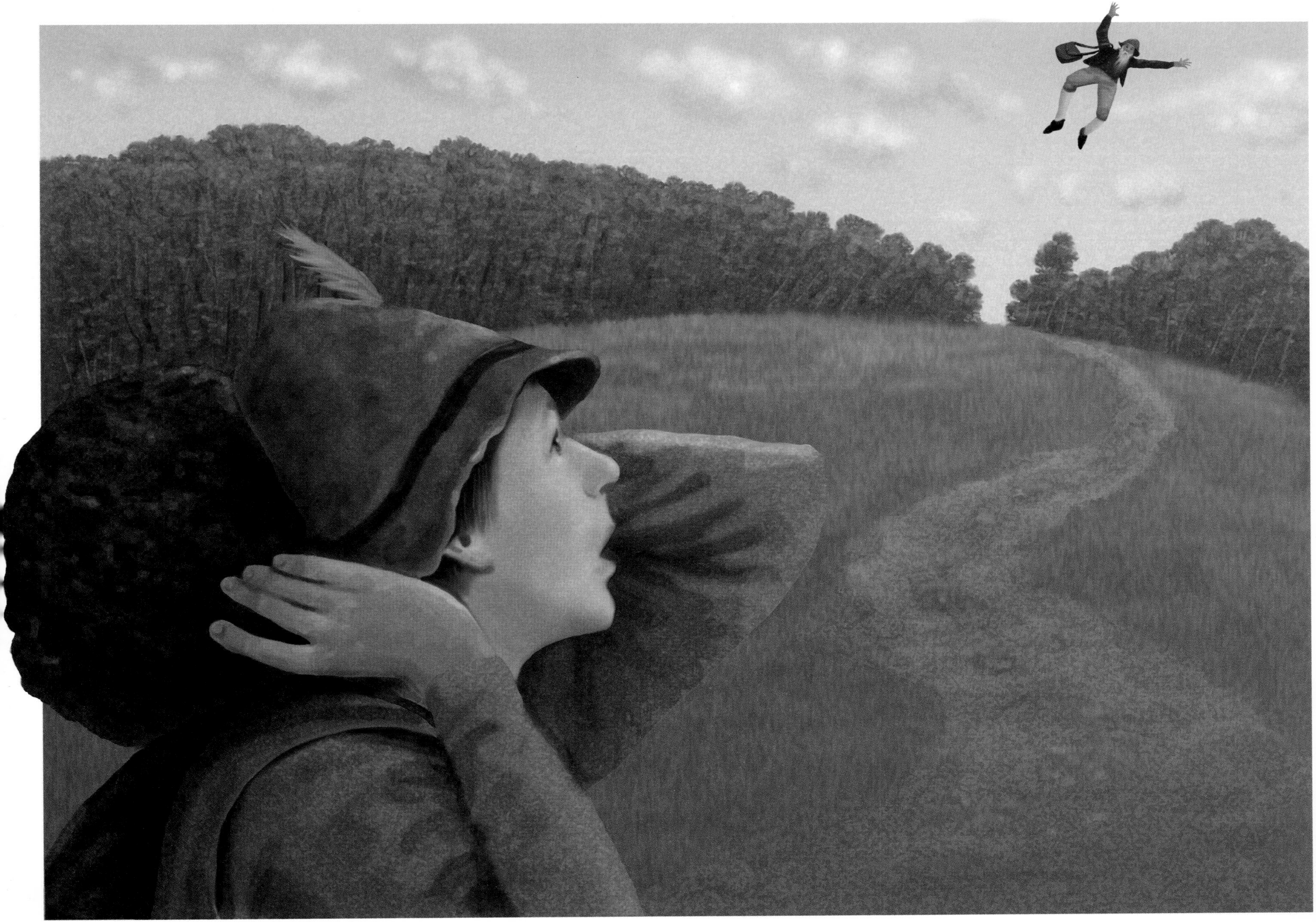

The son stared in amazement as his father floated into the sky like a downy feather in the breeze.

"Goodbye, Father!"

"Goodbye, Son!" the father said, as he disappeared into the clouds.

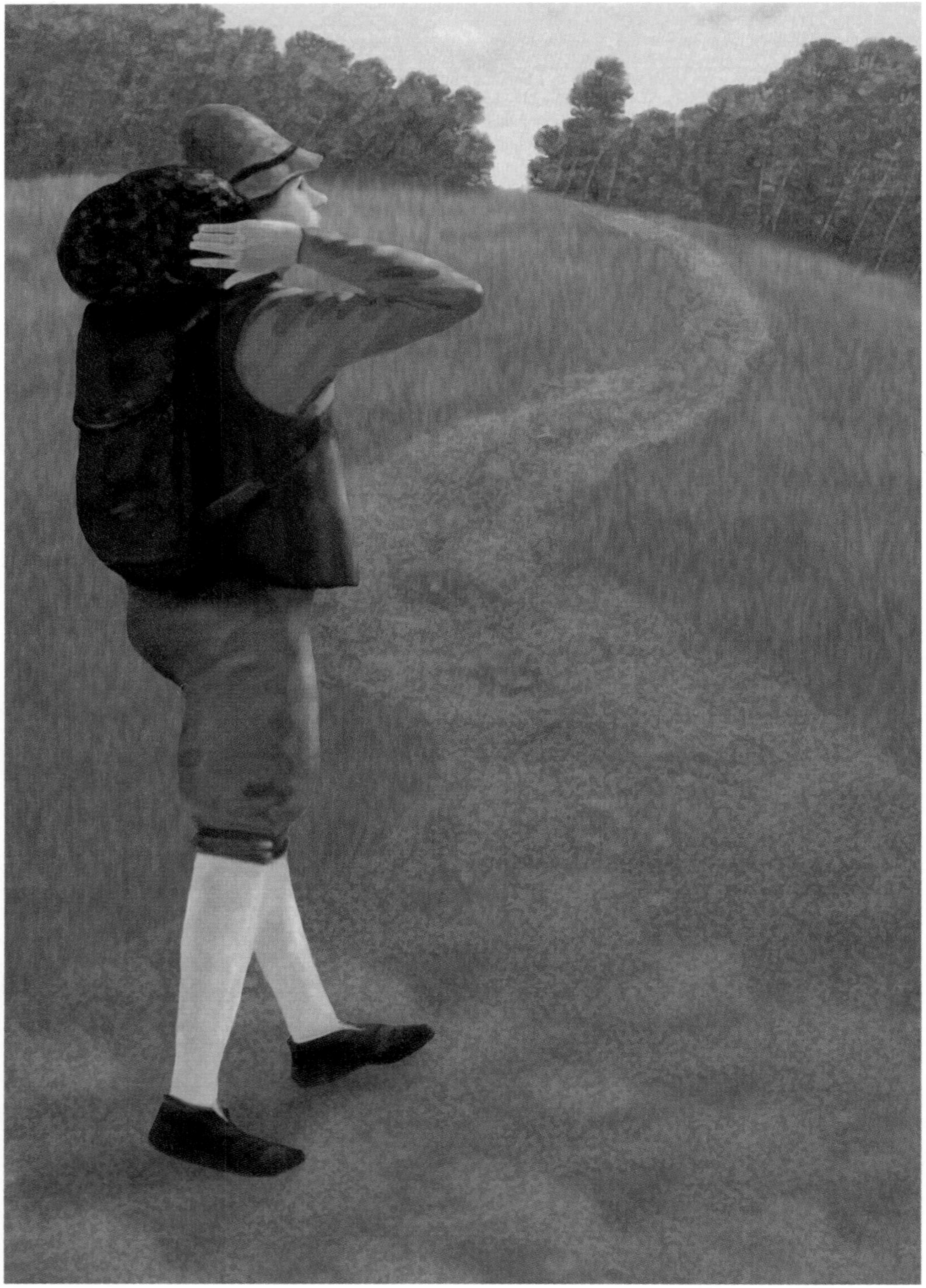

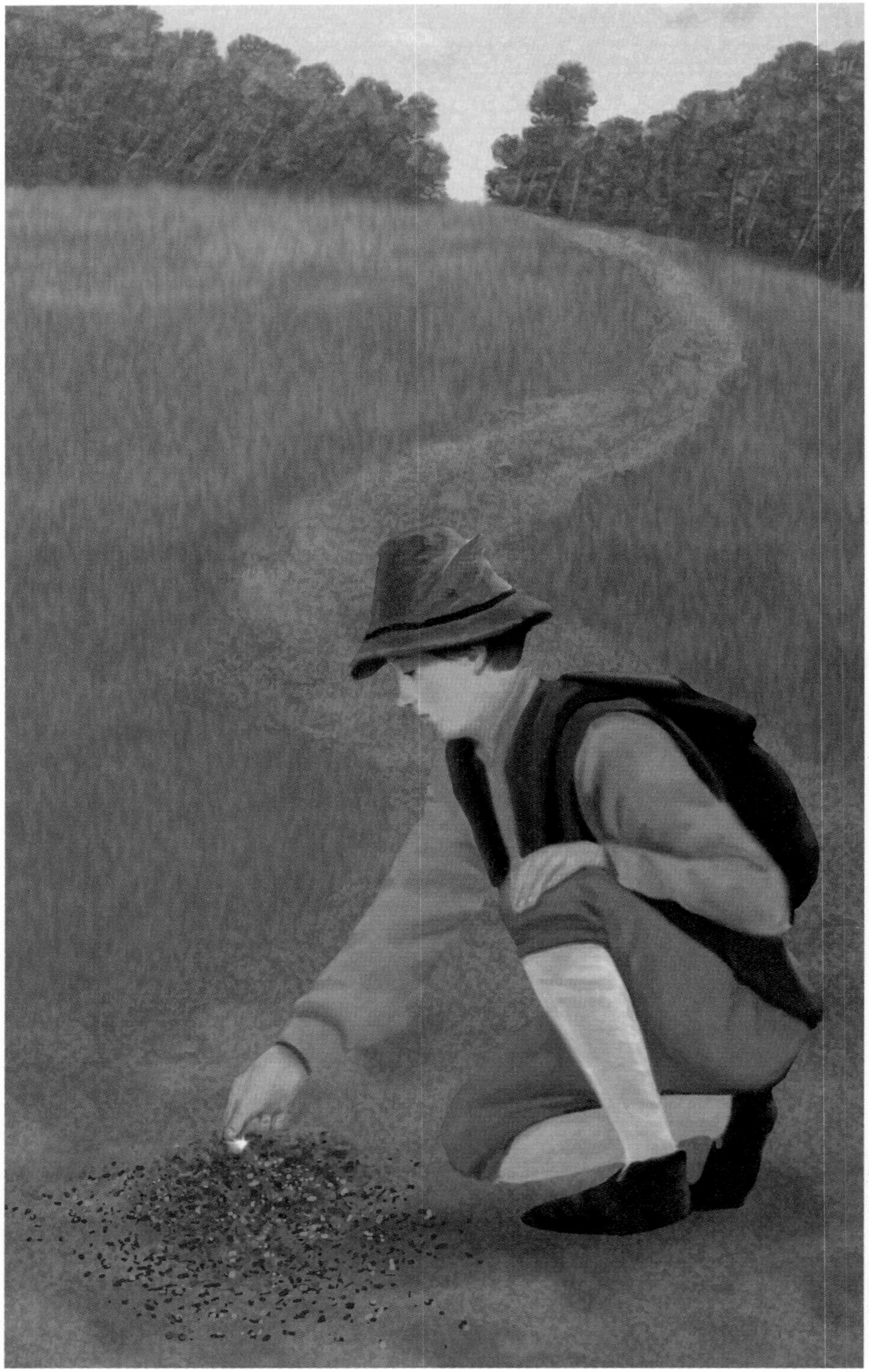

The son was left all alone on the road at the bottom of another steep hill with the heavy stone on his back. He took two steps. He stopped. He looked up at the hill. The son let the stone fall fom his back. The stone crashed to the ground and broke into hundreds of little pebbles.

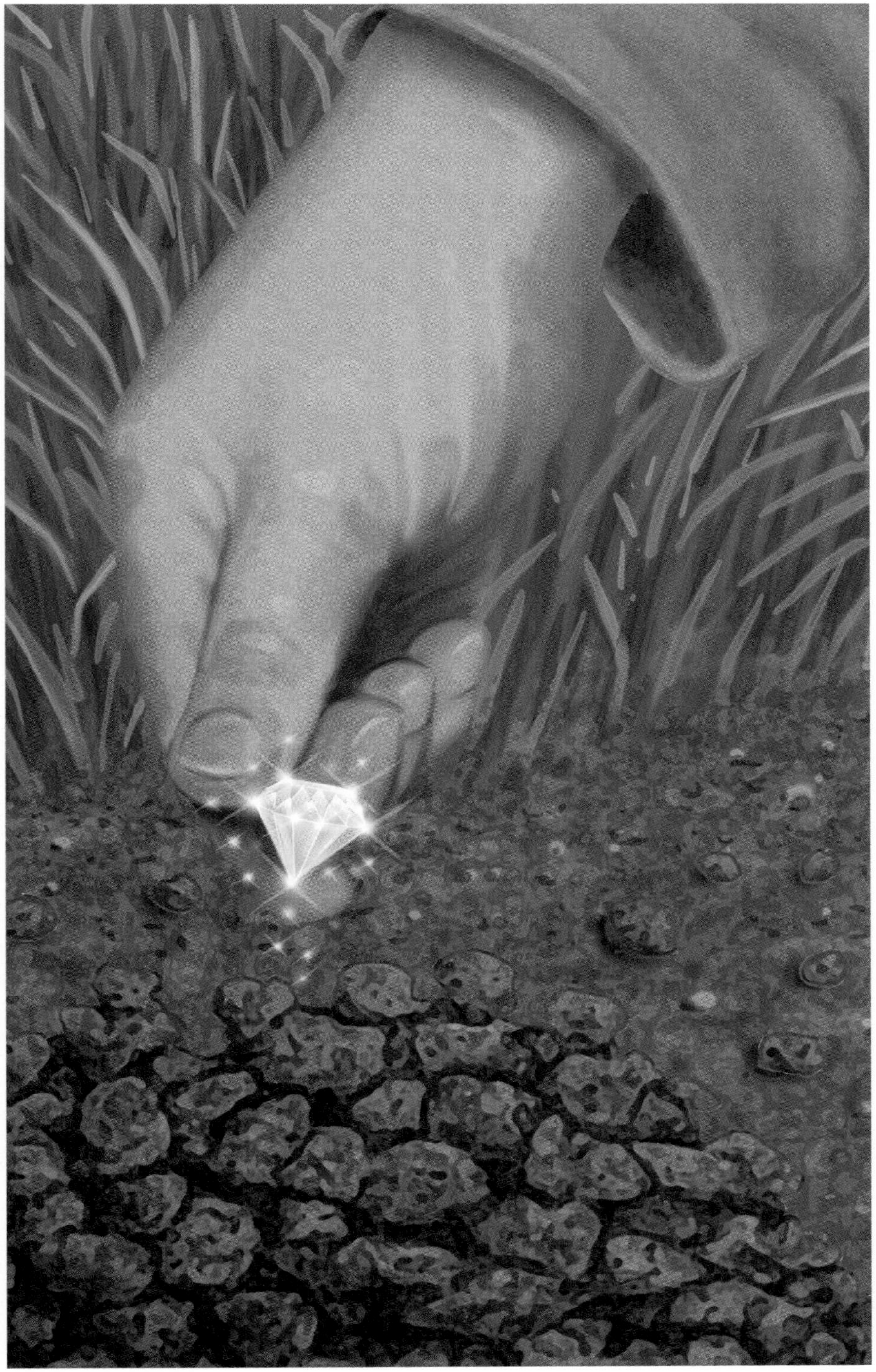

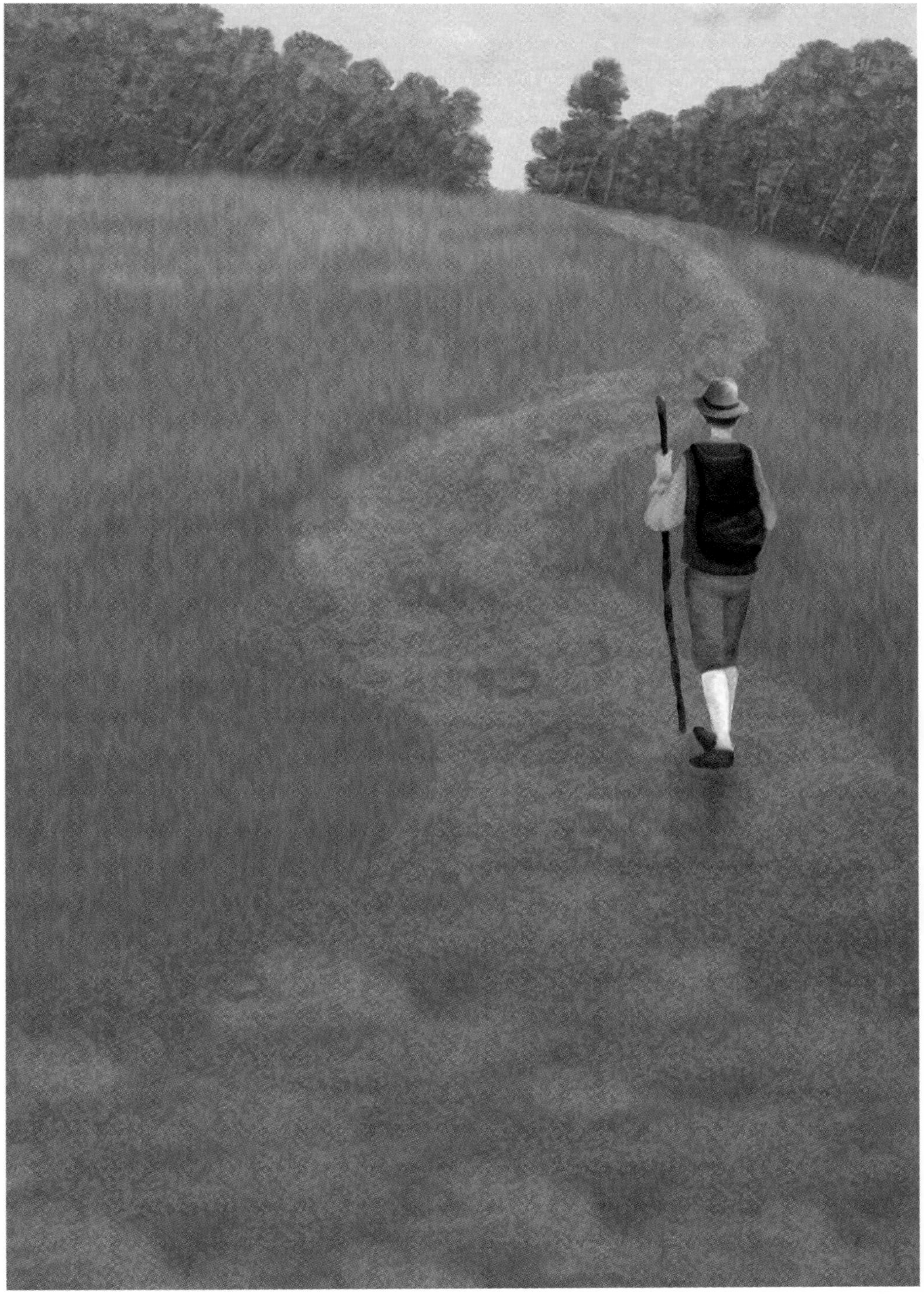

As the son looked, a sparkle caught his wondering eyes. It was a big beautiful diamond. He picked up the diamond and put it in his pocket. The son left the pile of pebbles behind and walked up the hill.

At the top he met a farmer's daughter. They fell in love and were married. Their life was rich, free, and happy, with many children who loved them.

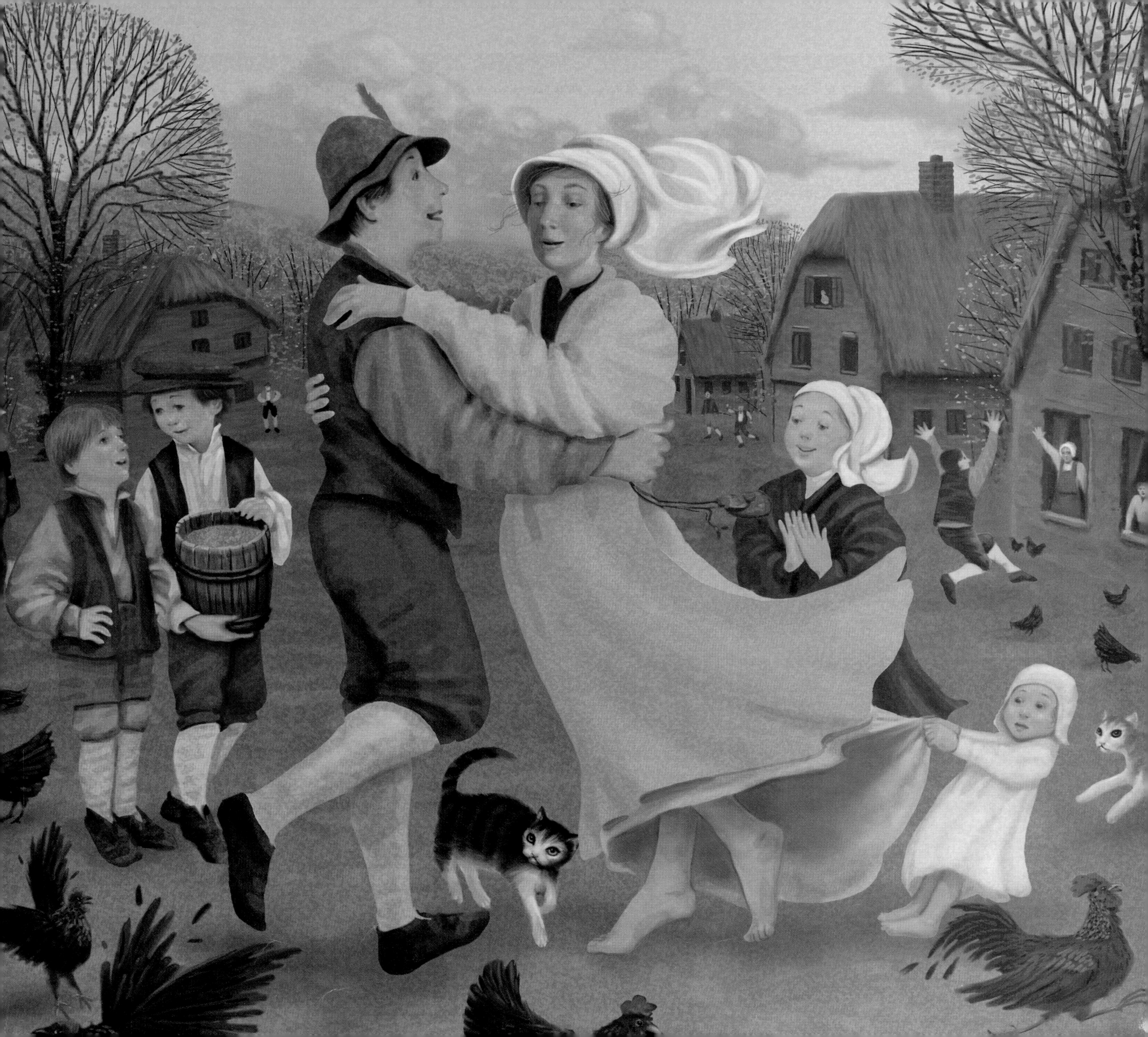